Merry Christmas, Matty Mouse

BY Nancy Walker-Guye

ILLUSTRATED BY Nora Hilb

North-South Books
NEW YORK / LONDON

It was the last day of school before Christmas. "Yippee!" cried Matty as he rushed out the door and leaped into the snow. He couldn't wait to get home.

Matty had two presents for his mother in his backpack. One was a recipe book with directions on how to make Christmas biscuits. The other present was a small box with six Christmas biscuits inside. Matty had spent the entire afternoon at school baking them. They were still warm and their smell tickled his nose.

I can't wait to give them to Mother, he thought excitedly. There will be three for her and three for me.

On his way home, Matty met Fitz. He was gnawing
bark from a tree.

"Hello, Fitz," Matty said cheerfully.

"Hello, Matty," said Fitz. He twitched his pink nose.
"What smells so good?"

"It's my Christmas biscuits," Matty said proudly, and he
took out the beautifully decorated box.

"Oh," cried Fitz, "I am so hungry. Do you have one to spare?"

"Of course," said Matty.

"Mmmmm. Wonderful!" said Fitz. "Much better than that scratchy bark. Thank you!"

"Merry Christmas!" said Matty as he continued home.

Further down the road Matty saw Jay pecking the hard frozen earth.

"Hello, Matty," Jay said as he found a tiny, shrivelled raspberry and gobbled it up.

Jay looks hungry, too, thought Matty. "Would you like a Christmas biscuit that I baked in school?" he asked.

"I certainly would!" cried Jay. "It's very hard to find anything to eat during the winter."

Jay ate the biscuit and pecked every crumb off the ground. "Thank you so much, Matty. Merry Christmas!"

"Merry Christmas to you, too," said Matty.

His backpack felt lighter on his shoulders. Hmmm, he thought, I had six Christmas biscuits, but I gave away two so now I have two for Mother and two for me. That works out just fine.

It was starting to get dark and Matty's feet were getting cold. He hurried home.

Matty was nearly there when he met Kika. She was
scratching frantically in the snow.

"What are you doing?" asked Matty.

"I'm trying to find my acorns!" cried Kika. She hopped
to another place and started digging. "I don't remember
where I hid them and my children are very hungry!" She
looked at Matty's backpack and asked hopefully, "You
don't have any acorns in there, do you?"

"No, I don't," said Matty, and he turned to leave.
Kika has two children, he thought. If I gave her three
Christmas biscuits, there would only be one left for
Mother.

Just then, Matty heard the squirrel children call, "Mother, where are you? Our stomachs are rumbling!"

Matty sighed. "I don't have any acorns," he said, "but I do have Christmas biscuits that I baked in school. Here is one for each of you."

"Thank you so much!" cried Kika happily. She snatched the Christmas biscuits and stuffed them in her cheeks so that she could carry them to her children. "Mewy Crifmaf!" she called.

She climbed up the tree and disappeared into her hole.

"Yes, Merry Christmas," murmured Matty.

Finally, Matty was home. He stood for a moment at the front door. There is only one biscuit left for Mother, he thought. Matty's whiskers trembled and his ears drooped with sadness. A stray snowflake landed on his nose.

The door opened a crack and Mother peered out.

"Matty!" she cried. "Why are you standing outside in the cold?" She put her arm around him and brought him into the warm house.

As soon as Matty stepped inside he began to cry. He told Mother how he had baked Christmas biscuits for her in school. Then he told her about Fitz, Jay, Kika, and her children. "Since they were so hungry," he said, "I gave them the biscuits that were meant for you. And now there is only one left."

Mother held him in her arms. "Matty, I am so proud of you," she said.

"Proud?" Baffled, Matty looked at Mother.

"Yes," said Mother. "It must have been very hard for you to share your Christmas biscuits. I don't mind at all that there is only one left for me. Everybody else just got one, didn't they?"

Matty nodded, his lip trembling. "Everybody but me."

"You haven't tried one yet?" asked Mother in surprise. "Well then, I'll make us a pot of cinnamon tea and we can eat the last biscuit together."

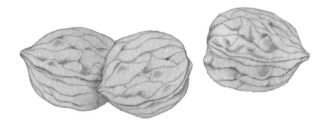

Matty and Mother sat together at the table, sipping
their cinnamon tea and sharing the last Christmas biscuit.
"This is delicious," said Mother. "Do you remember all
of the nuts that we gathered last autumn? If only we had
the recipe, we could make more of these wonderful
Christmas biscuits."

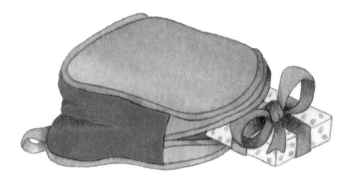

The recipe book! thought Matty. How could he have forgotten?

"I have another present for you," he announced.

He ran to his backpack and brought out the gift. "You may open it right away," he said.

"Two presents in one day!" exclaimed Mother. "Thank you so much!"

The next day Matty and his mother baked dozens of tasty biscuits. They invited Fitz, Jay, Kika, her children, and all their other friends to a joyful Christmas party. They all went home that evening with their stomachs full of Christmas biscuits and their hearts full of Christmas cheer.